THE LITTLEST PIRATE

NICHOLAS NOSH IS THE
LITTLEST PIRATE IN THE WORLD.
'YOU'RE TOO SMALL TO GO TO SEA,'
SAID HIS DAD. BUT NICHOLAS
IS BORED. VERY BORED.
'I'LL SHOW THEM,' HE SAYS.
AND WHEN THE FIERCE PIRATE
CAPTAIN RED BEARD KIDNAPS HIS
FAMILY, NICHOLAS SETS SAIL TO
RESCUE THEM!

Happy Cat First Readers

THE LITTLEST
PIRATE

SHERRYL
CLARK

ILLUSTRATED BY
TOM JELLETT

HAPPY CAT BOOKS

Published by
Happy Cat Books
An imprint of Catnip Publishing Ltd
Islington Business Centre
3-5 Islington High Street
London N1 9LQ

First published by Penguin Books, Australia, 2002

This edition first published 2006
3 5 7 9 10 8 6 4 2

Text copyright © Sherryl Clark, 2002
Illustrations copyright © Tom Jellett, 2002

The moral rights of the author and illustrator have been asserted

A CIP catalogue record for this book is available from the British
Library

ISBN 10: 1 905117 22 1
ISBN 13: 978 1 905117 22 2

Printed in Poland

www.catnippublishing.co.uk

Class No. .... Acc. No. 3227882

To Chrissy – go, girl! *S.C.*

For Hannah and Cassidy. *T.J.*

Chapter One

Nicholas Nosh, the littlest pirate in the world, wasn't allowed to go to sea.

'You're too small,' said his dad.

'When you're bigger you can go,' said his mum.

His older brother and
sister just laughed. They all
boarded their ship, the *Pig's
Breakfast*.

'Be good,' shouted his
dad.

'Eat your broccoli,' said
his mum. And they sailed
away to capture treasure.

Nicholas was left at home
with his babysitter, Gretta.

Gretta was very tall, with
long black plaits. Nicholas
barely came up to her knees.
Sometimes he climbed up
her plaits.

It was like climbing the
ropes on a ship.

Gretta loved to cook. She
especially loved puddings

and sweets, but sometimes her cooking was a disaster. Her cakes sank or her scones were as hard as rocks.

The spare pirate crew left behind didn't care. They ate all of Gretta's food and grew very fat and lazy. They were also supposed to be mending the spare ship, the *Golden Heart*, which had big worm holes in the hull.

Nicholas was bored. He'd practised with his cutlass and axe, and read his favourite book again, *The Biggest, Nastiest Pirates of all Time*. He'd played with all the treasure in the treasure room, but it wasn't the same as capturing it.

He was *so* bored that he decided to run away and join another pirate ship. 'I'll show them,' he said.

Nicholas packed his
cutlass and axe, and pulled
on his best leather boots.
Then he put on his pirate
hat and set off over the
hills.

Chapter Two

In the next town, Nicholas
found lots of ships tied up
along the waterfront. In
front of one ship Nicholas
saw a sign that read:
Wanted
Tough, mean pirates.

Apply on board.

Captain Scab.

Nicholas crossed the gangplank.

Captain Scab was sitting on a hatch cover, mending a sail. His trousers were

worn and his boots had no
laces. Old cannonballs and
bones littered the deck.

'I want to be a pirate on
your ship,' Nicholas said.

Captain Scab frowned at him. 'You don't look big enough.'

'I'm very good at sword fighting,' said Nicholas.

'I cut people off at the knees.'

'Can you fire a musket or a cannon?' asked Captain Scab.

'Er . . . no,' said Nicholas. 'But I'm great at swabbing decks and I can climb to the top of any masts.'

He noticed several rats sneaking around, picking at the bones. He gulped. 'Er . . . I can catch rats too . . . if I have to.'

'Hmmm,' Captain Scab
growled. 'I suppose I could
give you a go.'

Then he carried a large
barrel up from the hold.
'Ship's biscuits,' he said.

'Pick out all the weevils.'

Nicholas didn't like
crawly bugs but he wanted
to be a pirate. He picked up

a biscuit and banged it hard on the deck. All the weevils fell out.

'That's clever,' said Captain Scab.

Just then Gretta came running along the wharf. 'Nicholas! Nicholas!' she called.

Nicholas tried to hide behind Captain Scab but it was too late. Gretta had seen him.

'Nicholas!' Gretta puffed. 'You have to come home.'

'I don't want to,' said Nicholas. 'I've signed on with Captain Scab.'

'You can't!' wailed Gretta.

'Red Beard has captured your father and mother and brother and sister. I have a ransom note. Red Beard wants all of the treasure.'

'He can't leave yet,' said Captain Scab. 'He has to catch all these rats.'

'Sorry,' said Nicholas quickly. 'I have to save my family. Bye.'

He jumped off Captain Scab's ship and brushed down his clothes. Weevils and rats! Yuck!

Chapter Three

Nicholas and Gretta
climbed back over the hills.
In the cove lay the spare
ship, the *Golden Heart*. The
spare pirate crew were
busy loading cannonballs
and old muskets.

'I'll pack the food,' said
Gretta.

'I'll get a map and a
compass,' said Nicholas.

His dad had taught him
how to navigate. He hoped
he would be able to hold
the wheel to steer.

The sailors waddled
around the ship, closing the

hatches. Nicholas sighed.
They were too fat. They
would break the masts if
they climbed them. He
would have to unfurl the
sails.

Two hours later they set
off to search for Red Beard.
A strong wind filled the
sails and the *Golden Heart*
sped across the water.
Nicholas stood on a large

box at the ship's wheel,
steering west.

'Excuse me, Captain,' said
a pirate. His feet were
dripping wet. 'The ship is
still leaking.'

'Take the wheel,' Nicholas said. He went below to investigate.

Oh no! The lazy pirates had done a very bad job of mending the worm holes in

the hull. The ship was still leaking and water was sloshing in the hold. Barrels and boxes were floating everywhere. A large cheese bobbed past.

Nicholas raced up to the galley, where Gretta stood by the stove, stirring toffee.

'What can we do?' he said. 'We're sinking, and there's no tar left to fill the leaks.'

Chapter Four

'What about this toffee?'
said Gretta. 'I think this lot
will set.'

The toffee was bubbling
and thick. Nicholas carried
the pot below. He ordered
the sailors to bail out the

water and he quickly
spooned toffee into each
hole. The toffee set hard
and fast and the leaking
stopped.

'Yay!' cheered the sailors.

Nicholas was turning out to
be a very clever captain.

The *Golden Heart* sailed
so fast that it caught up
with Red Beard's ship by
the next morning.

The *Black Bog* was huge.
It had four masts and forty
cannons. It flew a black flag
with a red spider on it.

Through his telescope, Nicholas could see his parents and brother and sister. They sat on the foredeck, tied together with rope.

Red Beard stood over them. He was the biggest pirate Nicholas had ever seen. Four pistols hung from his belt. Spiders crawled in his long, red beard.

Nicholas felt very little.

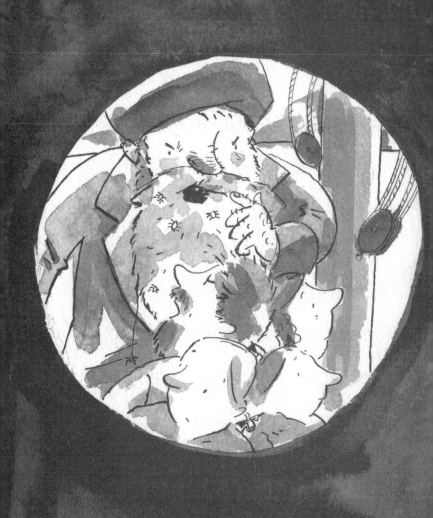

He shivered. 'We need to fire our cannons and try to bring down the masts,' he said, trying to be brave. 'Then we have to board and take the ship.'

But when he checked the cannonballs, he discovered that the lazy pirates had packed all the wrong shapes and sizes. None of them would fit in the cannons. All the muskets

were rusty and broken.

Nicholas went to the
galley where Gretta stood
by the stove, frowning into
a large pot. 'Maybe more
brown sugar,' she muttered.

Nicholas peered at the rows of bowls lined up on the table. They were all filled with horrible yellow sticky stuff.

'What are you cooking?' he asked.

'Caramel puddings. Some are too heavy, some are too runny. I don't know where I went wrong.'

Nicholas thought about how big the *Black Bog* was,

and how fierce Red Beard
looked. He wanted to cry,
but he was a pirate and
pirates are too tough to cry.

Chapter Five

As he stared at the bowls, Nicholas had a wonderful idea. 'Can I have these puddings?'

'You can't eat all of them,' said Gretta.

'I'm not going to. Help me

carry them up.'

In no time at all, there
was a big pile of caramel
puddings on the deck.

Nicholas sailed the *Golden
Heart* in close to the *Black
Bog*. Red Beard pointed and
laughed. All he could see
was Nicholas's hat bobbing
above the rail.

'Right, men,' said
Nicholas. 'Load the cannons
with the heaviest puddings.'

'We haven't had lunch,'
said one fat pirate.

'Why can't we eat these?'
said the fattest pirate of all.

His stomach and his double
chin jiggled up and down.

'They'll give you a
terrible tummy-ache,'
Gretta said.

The pirates thought
about the tummy-ache
they'd had from Gretta's
rock scones. They quickly
loaded up the heavy
puddings into the cannons.
'Fire!' yelled Nicholas.

One after the other,
puddings sailed through
the air and hit Red Beard's
masts and sails. The lazy
pirates were good shots and

two masts broke with loud
cracks.

'Load the runny
puddings!' Nicholas
shouted. 'Fire!'

The runny puddings splattered all over the *Black Bog*. The sails stuck together. The ropes were too slimy to hold. Best of all, the cannons fizzled out before they could be fired.

Red Beard's pirates slipped and skidded in the caramel. They couldn't stand up at all.

One pudding hit Red Beard smack in the chest.

Caramel dripped all over
him. All the spiders leapt
out of his beard and ran
away. Red Beard fell over
and stuck fast to the deck.

His legs and arms waved in the air.

Nicholas took his axe, grabbed a rope and swung across to board the *Black Bog*. His pirates followed, scrambling over the rails. They yelled and swung their cutlasses.

'Look out, you yellow-livered leeks!'

'Surrender, you soggy sacks of sausages!'

Red Beard's pirates tried to fight back. But their cutlasses slid out of their hands and their pistols were clogged with caramel. They were soon rounded up and thrown overboard.

Gretta cheered.

The fattest pirates picked up pieces of pudding and tasted them.

'Urrgh!' said one. 'Like old leather boots.'

'Bleuck!' said another.

'Like frog slime.'

Nicholas cut the ropes
around his family to free
them. Then he ran down
the stairs to the hold.

In a few moments he'd
chopped a hole in the
bottom of the *Black Bog*
and water began to rush in.

But while he was below, Red Beard had pulled free of the caramel. He was waiting for Nicholas, his cutlass ready.

Chapter Six

As Nicholas climbed the stairs, Red Beard shouted, 'I'll fix you, you little rat!' He stabbed at Nicholas.

But Nicholas was fast as well as little. Red Beard's cutlass clanged against

Nicholas's axe. He dodged
and dived, twisted and
turned. Red Beard swung
his cutlass and slipped in

the caramel. Then Nicholas
ducked in and chopped off
Red Beard's big toe.

'*Oooowwwwww!*' While
Red Beard was crying and
looking for his toe, Nicholas
ordered his pirates off the
Black Bog. 'It's going down
fast,' he said.

He swung back to the
Golden Heart, where his
family was waiting.

'Well done,' said his dad.

'You were very brave,'
said his mother.

His brother and sister
didn't say anything. They
were too amazed.

'I'm glad my puddings
were useful,' said Gretta.

She grinned. 'I think I'll make chocolate mudcakes next.'

Nicholas gulped. 'What about some nice meat pies for the crew?'

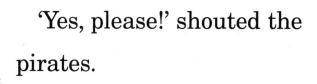

'Yes, please!' shouted the
pirates.

As the *Black Bog* sank,
the sea gurgled and bubbled.

Red Beard started swimming for the coast.

'It's a pity about Red Beard's ship,' said Dad. 'I need a new one since Red Beard has burnt mine. We'll just have to capture one on the way home.'

'What about this one?' asked Nicholas.

'Oh no,' said Dad. 'The *Golden Heart* is your ship now.'

'Then Gretta is my first mate,' said Nicholas. 'And I'm going to call my ship the *Golden Pudding*!'

From Sherryl Clark

The Littlest Pirate popped into my head while I was trying to write a BIG novel about pirates.

I love cooking new things but sometimes I have 'Gretta' disasters too!

From Tom Jellett

When I was a lot younger, my parents gave me and my younger sister a toy pirate ship. It had a pirate crew, real sails, wheels for when it wasn't sailing in the bath, and little spring-loaded cannons with tiny cannonballs.

It wasn't long before my mum took the cannons away from me because I kept firing the cannonballs at my sister. Perhaps using small puddings would have been safer.

The Princess and the Unicorn

Wendy Blaxland

No one believes in unicorns any more. Except Princess Lily, that is.
So when the king falls ill and the only thing that can cure him is
the magic of a unicorn, it's up to her to find one.
But can Lily find a magical unicorn in time?

Nobody is better at being bad than Buster Reed – he flicks
paint, says rude words to girls, sticks chewing gum under
the seats and wears the same socks for weeks at a time.
Naturally no one wants to know him. But Buster has a
secret – he would like a friend to play with.
How will he ever manage to find one?

When Anna Slept Over

Jane Godwin

Josie is Anna's best friend. Anna has played at Josie's house,
she's even stayed for dinner, but she has never slept over.
Until now...

Becky was cross with her little brother. 'If you don't leave me alone,' she said to him, 'I'll put a spell on you!' But she didn't mean to make him disappear!

Tom was given a gorilla suit for his birthday. He loved it and wore it everywhere. When mum and dad took him to the zoo he wouldn't wear his ordinary clothes. But isn't it asking for trouble to go to the zoo dressed as a gorilla?

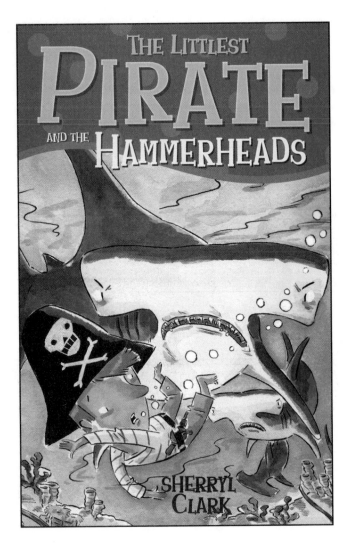

Nicholas Nosh, the littlest pirate in the world, has to rescue his family's treasure which has been stolen by Captain Hammerhead. But how can he outwit the sharks that are guarding Captain Hammerhead's ship?

Crystal longs to be a mermaid.
Her mother makes her a flashing silver tail. But it isn't like
being a proper mermaid. Then one night Crystal wears her
tail to bed...